Nothing Really Happens

Robert S. Gerleman

Productions

San Francisco, CA

First Edition – February 10, 2014

ISBN-13: 978-0615949666
ISBN-10: 0615949665

Gerleman, Robert S.
Author Site: www.robswriting.com

ALSO FROM ROBERT S. GERLEMAN:

DAMNED IF I DO, DAMNED IF I DON'T

For Jacob

NOTHING
REALLY
HAPPENS

"'Where are we going?' I asked. 'I don't know' he said 'just driving'. 'But this road doesn't go anywhere' I told him. 'That doesn't matter.' 'What does?' I asked, after a little while. 'Just that we're on it, dude.' He said."

— Bret Easton Ellis, Less Than Zero

CONTENTS

Educated Ice   1

Lover Dreamer Loser Sap   5

Socio-pathetic   9

Incessant Romantic   15

The Opportunist   21

Beguiled   25

Give and Take   35

Wayward   39

Banshee   43

Dopey   47

Madman   51

Kindred Spirits   57

Runner Runner   61

The Alpha   73

Silicon Man   77

Kind-of Heart   81

My Dissident Narcissist   85

Kissless and Careless   89

Enchanted   101

Acknowledgements

Author Interview

EDUCATED ICE

What first draws Karen to Paul is how much better he fills out a dress than she. Two muscled lumps, furled and snarling under red satin. Boyish shoulders keep the secret that his throat makes clear. Plum colored eyes demand attention over a spurious, close-shaven jaw. He is kind in manner, sweet in speech, and gentle towards everything. A black mane lays delicately on the nape of his neck, tenuous threads intermittently finding his mouth. Something worthy of a marble slab.

She watches quietly as several men at the bar follow the clicking of Paul's heels as he makes his way to the ladies room. She thinks about how strange it must be for him to have to choose which door to enter. A little blue man or a little blue woman—the only dis-similarity between the images being that of a small triangle.

Karen wishes she could fool them, as Paul has undeniably and quite brazenly done. To pass through the crowd as something other than who she is. To act the wolf for once would be a deliciously deceitful change.

"Another drink Miss?" The bartender points to her glass of ice.

Distracted by thought, she misses a beat.

"Miss?" he begs.

"Yes please, two limes."

The bartender grabs a fresh glass from the rack and she stops him, spinning the ice with her finger and kissing the end.

"Educated ice," she says with a smile and returns her attention to the bathroom doors. The limitation in choice seems impossibly finite to Karen. "God's will," she hears her mother echo. The drink arrives on a small white square that is already soaked. She doesn't touch it. She can't.

A scream rings out, waking her from thought.

"*HE*, WAS PISSING!" a woman yells, breaking through the door, "PISSING?" she seems to question. Several men crowd her then.

The group of spectators turn their attention to the door, the triangle, Karen's focus. Their clumsy, incoherent motions only further her fixation. They are barbaric: hair-laced arms, nostrils flaring and red with nicotine, mustaches wet from drink or drug or spittle, and nothing at all that reminded her of *him*.

Unable to contain herself, she joins the gathering by the door. The room floods with befuddled faces as they look up at the right angle just beyond the stall doors. A small window. An opened pane of glass with mere remnants of the creature that passed.

LOVER-DREAMER-LOSER-SAP

Wrote something on a bar napkin. Became an idea that launched a business. Used a bunch of buzz words like iterative and concatenate and dry powder. Got funding. Got an advisory board. Got a motorcycle. Got fired by my Best Friend.

Cinco de mayo, drunk. Crashed. Lost half a knee and slept in jail.

Took a job at a bookstore. Found a girl who cared. She left me. I drank a lot more.

Moved far north, went back to school, slept on a beach for three weeks while trying to find housing. Found another girl. It ended ugly.

Bartended at a pool hall. Regulars never tipped. Bouncers got knocked out. Cue ball broke a window on new year's eve. Owner only patches things.

Moved in with a close buddy. We stopped being close. Met a new girl. Fell in love. Moved in with her instead. Finally felt happy. Money ran thin. We got an apartment with another couple. Things fell apart. She left me and moved to the city.

Graduated. Didn't care.

Followed the last girl to the city and rekindled things. For a while, things were pretty alright. Spent a lot of time in parks with half-ers of wine and a blanket. Cooked for her. Played homemaker while she worked. Slowed down for a bit then floored it. Started hiding empty beer cans and wine bottles. Then she remembered she wanted a man—not the boy-wife I'd become—and lost interest. Left me for a co-worker. Maybe if I hadn't been so drunk, so often, so always.

She lives with him these days; *our* apartment now *theirs*...

Ex-Best-friend took me in. Started over. Started working. Started using heavy drugs.

Productive and assertive and speculative as fuck. Learned more, lived more. Moved at a pace I didn't think possible. Lost 40 pounds. Picked up Tennis, and Yoga, and the Gym at 3AM. Flossed twice a day. Started tanning. Read books. Smoked cigarettes. Stopped drinking and picking up calls. Forgot about most things.

The girl I fell in love with gets married and I feel sick. Not because I miss her, but because I couldn't care less. I've been emptied yet keep finding more to spew. More room to dig.

People try to help. Mostly just to watch. Comforted in knowing there exists a dismal me, standing over some balcony wondering if I'll make it. Someone tells me "Man, you aren't even in that deep of a hole, just reach up and pull yourself out." Silence. More smoke. "I mean, it's *your* grave, sit in it if you want to. How long is up to you."

No idea what to say, they're completely right. Scared to face my past I guess. More so to face a future without a reason to be held back.

SOCIO-PATHETIC

It's raining; she's in tears. Worried about the dampness falling from her loins: how it got there, how I got there. We remain motionless in the almost-dark, unable to hide from our mistake.

The glass door is slightly ajar. A small pool forms at the crack. I watch it expand and shallow, wondering if it will reach me.

She's found solace in the bathroom. Tightly shut away. Something falls, breaks, fills the sink. And I can feel her holding back the screams.

In love? We're not even in lust. A brutal joke with a punch-line to the face. Do I leave? Where's my jacket? I don't even know where the front door is.

"You gotta' go..." she says through the door, "...just..." she's drawing a bath, "...I'll call you, okay?"

And I'm leaving, my jacket by the exit, her roommate tucked safely away someplace, an unopened beer on the counter, I take it down easy, surprisingly sated. I'm still drunk and as I step outside, the rain fizzles. Sun burns through a weaker cloud and I'm spinning. Wading through the dryness of it. The heat of the spell.

Short lived, the rain resumes. It's worse now.

She won't call. Don't want her to. I should probably feel terrible but don't feel much of anything. Not for a while now. This city has bested me. The apex of the peninsula towering over its golden coast and copper bridge. The edge of the world if you squint just right. Or the fog rolls back from its hilly hiding places.

The 49 rushes by. Van Ness. Its miserably cold but I'm sweating nonetheless. It's these goddamn hills. Nob and Russian and Telegraph, Rincon, Twin Peaks, Mount Sutro and Davidson. 47 fucking hills with peaks from a hundred to a thousand feet, all within 50 square miles. I should hate this but then I remember to breathe and everything smells oh-so-sweet. Sewer steam and all.

Head south on Polk Street. Swan Oyster Depot already has a line. Bar on the next block is open. They're always open. Pretty sure they start pouring at

6AM but it's an hour past so I'm fairly certain everything will work out.

Dead end off Frank Norris Street. An alleyway really. Big golden tooth hangs above the door. It's dark as hell but I keep my sunglasses on. Order a Jameson-neat and a pint of something seasonal. **The bar is surprisingly full.** This girl is mouthing off at the other end of the rail. She's blonde and tall and built like a fighter but still shaped like a woman. She makes her way down the bar, totally blitzed, hoping to sucker another drink out of someone. Maybe "sucker" is the wrong word, more like pity. She gets to me:

"You got a black eye or something?" She nods at my shades. I take down the Jameson. She's tracing the tumbler, finds the pint, grabs for it. I get her hand in time.

"Something like that," I say and she goes limp.

"You're funny," she smiles, "You hear the one about the woman at the grocery store?"

I stay silent, knowing she'll continue.

"So this woman is at a grocery store right? She's got lettuce and bread and a can of peanuts, and the guy in line behind her says 'You're single, aren't you?' and the woman says 'Well, yes. But how did you know?' and the guy looks her dead in the eyes right, not missing a beat, and says 'Because you're ugly as fuck!'"

She starts laughing at herself then gets up, sits next to a dumb looking guy with a not-so-vintage t-shirt on, and starts the game again.

***

Still raining. It's a redhead this time. I don't think we fucked. I get up before her, run to the pisser and leave one. There's a bump of white powder left in my bag, I shake it onto a swimsuit mag and dig it up with the end of a torn pack of zigzags. I'm up. There's a bottle of Maker's Mark on top of the fridge, some ice, a flat bottle of club soda. And I'm finishing the drink when I hear her sneaking the bathroom door shut. The water roars. Maybe we *did* fuck. The TV is on and I take a seat, find the swimsuit mag again and start twisting up a joint while smoking a cigarette.

She comes out as I'm fingering the ashes and asks, "Coffee babe?" her hair wet and up, a towel covering her bust, pleading to be unfurled.

I make another drink, start the coffee pot for Red. Return to the couch. Start flipping through bullshit as the steam builds in the maker, bubbling tannins and faux chocolates and hazelnut from the powdered shit I dumped in.

I smoke more. She's dressed. Tells me to "get-the-fuck-up". I do so, languidly.

We drive up to a Trader Joe's with the windows down. She says the tint makes her look suspicious.

12

Rain pools on the sill, the armrest, my sleeve. We pick up beans and red meat and an avocado, tortillas, some beer.

She tells me about something called a "sangria swirl" which uses industrial strength margarita slush and sangria spun over an orange slice that I "just *have* to try".

We make a quick stop, kill a round of swirls, and head back to her place where she immediately starts cooking.

I'm back on the couch I can't seem to escape, flipping through shit on TV. Roll another joint. She pours me some beer in a frosty glass from a frosty quart. The smell of spiced beef fills the apartment and my stomach tightens.

She brings me a plate, one for herself. We laugh awhile about politics and religion and how far away from us they seem to be. Then she starts wailing about her ex.

Revealing herself to be both damaged and shame-less I feel tender and decide to play along. Full from the meal, she keeps feeding me cigarettes and booze and kisses and I begin to feel locked–in a strangely pleasant sort of way–so I stay and start to wonder if I'll ever leave. Knowing all the while that I must.

***

The rain has let up and I find myself speeding

down the interstate in a car too small for three. I want the girl who's driving but her friend is in my lap. Cheap whisky chases us towards a sleepless night; legs under me, over me, up in the air. Eventuality rears its complacent head and I am fixed. Her hips become part of me, gliding knowingly across my thighs. I hesitate. She squeezes first. Everything stops, and the motion and speed and reverence of it all rush into me. Engorged beneath her I am helpless. The driver swerves and I'm throbbing. They look at me—completely independent of one another—and we laugh as traffic comes to a stop.

INCESSANT ROMANTIC

I just fell in love with a girl on the corner of Sutter and Hyde. Maybe it's the way she taps her fingernails against her teeth while trying to decide if either the plums or peaches outside the corner market are even remotely fresh enough to eat. Or it could be the gentle and frequent shift of weight between her hips as she moves. Or maybe it's just nostalgia.

I annex one of the metal lawn chairs they keep out front for smokers, newspaper readers, and early morning drinkers to relax and indulge and reminisce about how things used to be. Then I lose focus, as those delicate hips begin to whisper.

She is near defeat and resumes tapping her teeth, then stops suddenly and with a delighted gasp extends her reach to select a single suitable plum. Tiny yellow heels dart up. Relentless calves, hearty from the hills and the life-giving haunches that surely lay beneath that thin blue dress. The row of withered market denizens beside me leans forward in a well-practiced leer, all of them wishing as strongly as I: If only there were a breeze…

I light a smoke, breathe deep, and join the panel of elderly in their haze of muddled memories. Above me, a green-grey-white fire escape that couldn't possibly work trails up to a bay window I used to sit comfortably behind, surveying a project across the street, erecting something new from the rubble of our city's condemned. I remember wondering what would become of me, us, this. A world where construction has grown beyond mere mechanization. So much so, that the presence of mankind will seem superfluous if not irrelevant were it not for the physical necessity of the structures to which it is bound.

And I watch as even now they continue to build: The massive tonnage of rebar hooked to tenuous lines of cable reaching up from under the arm of a great, iron beast-on-wheels, vacillating precariously above its tamers like the sword of Damocles, waiting to fall from the godlike fingers of an emotionless machine.

Wraiths of guilt peer down, assuring me that my little studio of old hasn't forgotten. How the floors rumbled when the bar beneath had a crowd. The sound of the 2, 3, and 76 scraping under the wire with its captured souls in tow.

"Fuck!" I bark, and drop the cluster of embers that's bitten me.

The sun has dropped early, the sidewalk loungers are gone, and I can either sit here by the warmth of my faded memories or follow that blue dress as it slinks onto a stool at the bar next door.

I walk in, she's there. All green eyed and blondish and thankfully sitting alone. She has slender shoulders and sharp-ridged collar bones that just scream WOM-AN! I want to rest my chin in the crevasse of her bosom and wiggle my way up and across the silhouette of her shoulders, pausing to kiss every available space on that tall, craning, neck.

"I'm Jack," I say with strange confidence. "May I buy you a drink?"

"You may," she says and holds out her hand, "Michelle."

I take her hand and try my best to contain a goofy-looking smile.

We order drinks. Beer for me, vodka-soda for her. I grab at my pint too quickly and spill the head over my fingers. The tender snorts a half-laugh and turns back to the till. Michelle's emerald eyes look up and off then back to me and when our lines of sight connect I can see clearly all the heartache they've bestowed before mine.

She is gorgeous and I am weak. But I am not overlooking my weakness, just allowing it to be. Allowing me to live on and enjoy what is present and kind. Like green eyed blondes, and pints spilling foam, and a bartender who's seen it all before. All the while remembering that this life, much like the next, is not guaranteed.

"You smoke?" She says, fingering two from her purse.

We head out front. She lights hers, then mine, and takes a voluptuous pull. "Where are you from, Jack?"

"California."

She laughs, "I meant *where* in Cali, hon."

"Northern," I say, keeping it vague.

She relents, "Okay, well what does Jack from Nor-Cal do?"

I can barely focus. All I want to do is hail a cab, escort her home, and find out what's under that dress. Then, with some sort of knee-jerk reaction, I finally respond, "Nothing," with as serious an expression as I can muster.

She studies my face a moment, searching for cracks in the veil. Her eyebrows crop up and frame her face nicely. Those soft eyes and full lips blossoming over a virginal pallor turned pink from the day's sun. I finally let loose that goofy grin and she begins to laugh.

"You are something else, you know that?"

We toss the smokes and head back inside to finish

our drinks. I order another round and we start talking. Really talking. I find myself telling her things I usually keep to myself. She maintains a smile, seems happy. I listen to her with genuine enthusiasm, truly eager for more. Drinks find our hands over and over. Each new ring on the bartop takes another place, another person, another minute of our youth, yet we are blissful as they evaporate into mere things we've left behind.

Without warning the lights come on and the bar wants us out. She offers me another cigarette but finds she only has one left and we share it out front.

"You wanna' get outta here?" I say between drags.

Michelle looks at me with her head tilted. The way a puppy does when you're making faces at it. She is waiting for another grin, which I give her.

"You're bad," she says and tosses the smoke. "How 'bout you walk me home?"

We start walking and as the bar dissolves behind her she grabs my arm, finds my hand. It's a perfect night for a walk. Everyone is either inside partying or never came out in the first place. I love how desolate it seems.

There is a strange openness to the streets of San Francisco. The streets are large and sprawling like a metropolis but peppered with little walk-ups and mom-and-pops that are reminiscent of little beach towns like Santa Cruz or Santa Barbara. It is a conglomerate of big and little city charm. And with

Michelle pinned to my flank, I couldn't be more content.

For a moment I imagine she is someone else. Someone I once loved. I imagine all the late night walks I'd taken with someone else's hand in mine. How happy it made me, warm or cold, rain or clear, starlit sky or cloudless sun. How we'd talk about her day, I'd tell her of mine. We would tell each other our dreams. She'd hug my forearm and kiss at my ear.

When we reach the steps up to her apartment building she stops short of the gate and turns to me, "I had a really great time tonight, Jack." Then she takes a step backward up the stoop, our shoulders level to one another. I say to myself "Fuckit." Then to her, "Mind if I kiss you?" She brings a hand to her mouth, pauses barely, and starts tapping her teeth.

THE OPPORTUNIST

I don't know how the conversation started but I liked where she was going with it:

"So this dude comes up to me, the bar is packed, we're at some posh pub downtown, and he tells me he's a doctor—which I only half-believe."

I finish what's left of my vodka-soda and order a fresh pair for the two of us.

"'What do you do?' he asks me all fake-like and I tell him some bullshit about starting work at an art gallery I saw opening up on Sutter and Powell."

"You aren't cocktailing anymore?"

The drinks arrive and she asks the tender for a few more limes.

"Cocktailing?" she laughs, "only with you sweetie."

We each take a heavy pull on our glasses.

"So he's buying me these cider beers right? We get pretty shitty."

"Where were you guys at? Top-cider or something?"

"Yea, Top-cider."

"Cute spot."

"It's pretty *alright*," she stops to squeeze the limes then licks her fingers. "Anyway we're getting shitty on the cider for like, ever, and I let him take me home, expecting something boring but whatever."

"You're such a slut, Karen"

"We end up in bed—fuck you by the way—and he goes down on me. Terrible. His little lizard tongue darting all over."

"Typical."

"Then he like, stops all of a sudden and wipes his mouth and says, 'You down for some crazy?'"

"Duh."

"So he leaves the room super quick, comes back with this old-school doctor's bag."

"So he really is a Doctor?"

"Guess so," She smiles crookedly, "anyway he opens it, takes out this strap-on. A massive, glorious, mother-fucker. He hands it over all weakly and shit, bends over the footboard, and just waits there wagging

22

his tail."

"How do you always get yourself into this kinda' shit?"

She finishes her drink and looks off as if trying to recall some distant memory.

"I stole the bag," she laughs. "Wanna' see it?"

*BEGUILED

Paul Foster

What I thought was going to be my greatest piece of work, the thing that set me apart from the rest, my friggin' Gatsby, has turned out to be a bigger disaster than I ever could have imagined. I spent the last three years, two months and thirteen days writing a Novel that will probably end my marriage, definitely shake up my career, and more likely than not threaten my life.

From the first page I knew that I had made a mistake. There was no fixing it. It couldn't be reworked, it couldn't be rewritten. Too volatile to be fucked with. And the story within had finally come to an unavoidable close.

"The End" I type with pink index fingers. A brief feeling of satisfaction before scrolling back to the beginning. The credits to my life story in reverse.

File, print.

A screen full of options I don't care to understand appears.

At the bottom I am given a choice. OK, or Cancel. I wish for a third option. An "I Guess So" button.

A polite but alarming tone arises. An error: Printer Not Responding. Even my computer is against me.

I try twice more until the spirits living in my DeskJet from sometime in the mid-nineties finally wake from their slumber and begin to howl. It screeches and bangs and claps about. An orchestra tuning goes silent, waiting on a green, flickering conductor.

Ink covered pages start spewing into the plastic tray and I cringe as the stack grows taller and taller. The more that is there, the more there is to detest. More of me exposed.

"What's the worst that can happen?" I ask the monitor.

It stares back blankly.

"Vikki is going to kill me."

Vikki is my Agent, best friend, and wife in no particular order. A combination that sounds ideal at first but eventually rings true to all those old adages we pretend are generalizations. She has been anticipating the coming of my second novel for years without getting so much as a glimpse of content. Why haven't I told her? Why haven't I let my better half, my compatriot, my representation, in on the secret?

Well, it's a matter of fiction versus non-fiction.

What was supposed to be a novel has ended up as more of a memoir. Of course that is more or less always the case in my opinion. And I haven't told Vikki about the change. Just like I haven't told her that this second piece of publishable work—the one almost finished printing—is about the affair I've been having outside our marriage.

"Job Done," my printer alerts as the title page finds its final resting place atop a two-inch stack of deceit, destined for retribution. The top corner reads:

Paul Foster

1560 Lincoln Ave

Eugene, OR

Then there is an obnoxious word count in the upper right, and a flimsy title somewhere in the mid-dle. All things subject to change.

It is an irrefutable truth that I have fallen in love with someone other than my wife. That many nights I lurk about the black city streets, thinking of how happy I am without her. But it hasn't always been this way.

Vikki has become reserved, sedentary. Nothing like she was when I married her. She used to be adventurous. She used to be spontaneous. She used to be rare. But I'm not going to try and justify my wrong doings by pointing a finger at her maturing depression. Because that is my fault too. I wasn't driven into someone else's arms by some wrong done unto me. I sprinted at them full speed and without regard.

Something in me wants a taste of strange. Maybe I always wanted it. But I never meant to fall in love. And I most certainly didn't intend to write about it.

In my first novel I named all my fictional characters after real people in my life. There was a love interest named Vikki, a best friend named Mark, a protagonist named Paul. All things I have in my own private world. But this book, this second book, is different. It deals with people that truly exist, truly matter. And for that reason I have decided to choose names in a more random fashion. I used mixtures of famous celebrities, or variances of my favorite authors, or some generic clerk's nametag. I wanted to feel detached from them all somehow. And so I did. There would have been no way I could have wrote it had I not.

So I wrote about a wife named Paris, a protagonist named Nathan Ames, and a mysterious lover. A lover who's name had to be disguised most of all. So, out of irony, I named him Elle.

"Honey?" Vikki calls from the front door.

"I'm in the office."

"Any pages in there?" Her keys drop onto the kitchen counter as she walks knowingly out of ear-shot. She is expecting the same mechanical answer I always give her. Another lie.

I had successfully kept her in the dark as to my progress since the beginning. Downtown at McMenamin's Café alone, roundtrip train tickets to nowhere, midnight typing under a flickering television. Every attempt at proving I'm the tormented, spiraling, yet impervious author that I so desperately strive to be.

Vikki knows better. She knows I am just a lost boy at heart. Someone that can't make the mark on society that he wants to. Someone caught between hard places.

Her initial attraction to me was out of sheer pity. She saw me as this fixer-upper she could invest in and then turn for a profit: Money, love, babies. But I have yet to give her any of those things.

In the beginning, it was just lust. A deep, weighty, lust that lasted longer than either of us expected. And gradually my bubbly, carefree Vikki turned into the scowl lipped Victoria with her mother waiting in the mirror.

"*Actually* Vik, I *do* have something."

"What?" She yells over a blaring television.

"I said…" and then reconsidering, scribble something on a post-it and head out to take my now imperative deliberation for a walk. She probably won't even notice I'm gone.

Victoria Foster

"Paul?" I call to an empty office and a closed door. Did I imagine his presence when I first arrived? I wouldn't put it passed me. I've just returned from my mother's and all I can think about is how much of a "what have I you done for me lately?" kind of parent she is.

I went to see her this afternoon for no particular reason and thoughtfully brought along a bundle of lilies. I knew she wouldn't thank me, she never does, but I continue to buy her gifts just the same. Not in hopes of gaining the appreciation I so sorely desire, but—and in a completely unselfish kind of way–for my own personal fulfillment. To feel good about being good. About being me.

"Paul?" I call again in a more feverish tone and walk through the kitchen to his office door where I find a note stuck to the knob.

V –

Went for a walk. Be back with dinner.
Chinese? Call if you want something else.

– P

I think Paul has been acting strange lately. I say "I think" because I haven't really been paying much attention to him over the past few months. Things have been beyond overwhelming. Work is exhausting (seeing as it is our sole source of income) and Paul has become increasingly elusive.

I love him though, I really do. But even when I say it in my head it feels like I am justifying it to myself. Does he do the same, I wonder. And what's with the closed door? He never used to pen himself up in his office. I bet he's got the shutters drawn and all the lights off, Googling himself and quoting Hawthorne.

Maybe if I tidy things up in there he will pick up a little positive energy and turn things around. Plus, it's a good excuse to see what that *little man* is hiding in there.

Hopeful for words, I gently press the door, purposefully encouraging the dry joints to creak.

I am surprised when I see how bright everything is. Not only are the shutters open, but the windows themselves. Everything is organized and put away. Nothing like the quintessentially frustrated and lazy writer I have come to live, with.

And there it is, sitting plainly on top of his printer.

"That sand-bagging, bastard."

Paul has been claiming "writers block" in some form or another for longer than I can remember. And all this time he has been silently pumping out pages upon pages.

Too confused to think and too frustrated to care I let it dawn on me: I am completely alone in the apartment.

I go to my purse and unzip a small side-pocket to grab my one-hitter. Paul hates that I smoke. He is the only author I've ever signed that doesn't get high.

A couple of shakes gets my lighter working.

The green sprouts glow orange and concentric circles swarm through to my lips. I let go and take a deep breath, holding in solid, milky, vapor as it burns.

A tickle jumps up. A cough rings out. A slow, muted brain ambles to a stop.

I kick off my shoes and sprawl out on the plush leather couch in our living room. With my eyes vaguely open, I feel a smooth wave of heat and exhaustion. My eyes close, a moment, coaxing forward my dreams.

At first, things that please me: discovering a gem in my slush pile, launching a new author, exposing something wonderful to the world, Paul. Paul and his deceit. That sneaky little…

A cracking sound in the freezer breaks my haze. The cubes of ice scatter into their collection tray like dice on a hardwood floor and it calls me closer. Closer to the rocky-road I know has been sitting there since two nights prior when I brought it home for Paul and I, but Paul didn't take a single bite, leaving me to finish alone. A trait that's unfortunately made its way to our bedroom.

The large metal platter we keep in the top cabinet above the fridge has an oversized serving spoon lying sharply across it. I have to have it. Almost as much as it has to have me. Something *has* to have me.

I take a few disappointing bites, trash the carton, and rush to the bathroom to wash my face and remove the melted mess that remains of my morning beauty.

Nothing is more aptly titled than facial cosmetics. They tell it like it is. *Concealer* of one's blemished self. *Foundation* for those who lack. *Blush* for those who can't. *Lip Gloss* for the few without. *Shadow* for eyes too honest.

A soft white robe hanging on the bathroom door falls on my shoulders. My hair drawn up and bath drawn out, I slip into the kitchen to uncork a bottle of white. I take a long deserved swallow until the glass is drier than the wine.

"Maybe some reading material?" I ask myself and open Paul's office. Still there, all alone, that thick cut slab of brain meat, just waiting to be violated.

I drop my robe to the floor. Submitting myself over the lacquered mahogany desk, drawing blood to my lips. Forcing, taking, stealing something away.

I grab the quiet stack, and scamper back to my bath, along with my glass, and step naked into the hot pool.

Settled, I begin. The manuscript:

Kissless and Careless
A novel by,
Paul Foster

*Originally published as "Two-Sided Triangle" in the *Toyon Literary Journal* 2012

GIVE AND TAKE

"Like that makes a difference," she says between drags.

"I've seen it happen."

"Yea, in the movies maybe."

A fevered mist spins from her lips.

"I'm just saying."

She stares off. A beat goes by.

"It's all you boys ever think about."

"What, getting high?"

"*High* is ambiguous."

"So?" I say, confused.

She turns to me.

"It's all a high. Sex, drugs... rock and roll," her tongue sticks out, fingers in the air, mocking. We laugh.

"Violence?"

She smiles, "That too," and steps on her cigarette.

"You know I love you, don't you?"

Her smile flattens and she comes to me, covers me, her hips enveloping mine. She kisses all over my face, strategically avoiding my mouth. Her hand guides mine to her neck and she squeezes. Everything grows tighter. My breath escapes me though it is she who is constricted.

I gnaw on her bottom lip. She moans softly. My jaw locks and I can feel an inaudible shriek. The pulse in her lips flows over my tongue. Salty cast-iron. The freezing bricks behind us begin to melt. I'm sweating so bad I can smell it. Her hands are cold on my back and the glassy beads roll between her feathery fingers.

"You know I love you, right?" I ask again.

She shrugs and those fingers disappear beneath her plaid pink skirt.

"Please," she begs in a whisper, her eyes red-white and barely blue.

"Here?"

"Please."

I don't want to. I never want to. But this is some-thing that had sunk its venomous teeth into us from the beginning, and I so desperately need her love right now. There's just no other way.

My hand finds a place along the side of her face and holds there a moment.

Then it makes a fist, and comes down hard.

*WAYWARD

Several stops pass with no riders. Stop, door opens, air. Stop, door opens, screech, whistle. Stop, stop, stop, and then one comes. A girl.

"Trisha!" She spoke her name as if she'd won something. One of those overly engaging, awkwardly enthusiastic type of people who are more interested in what *they* have to say than what you do in return. She likes me though, I can tell that much.

Trisha is an artist on her way to pick up one of her paintings she left in Oxnard that was going to be reprinted for a buyer in Germany. An arbitrary complexity that I don't care to understand. There's a calmness to her attitude that I admire. A sort of indifference that makes her unbelievably likeable.

"Jon Fowler," she reads the fake name on my bracelet aloud. I nod in agreement.

My real name is Fletcher. Fletcher Stevenson. But I have been using Jon for years now. Jon is mordant, convivial, limpid. He acts without concern for anything but himself. He knows only indulgence and opulence. He is flamboyant and obnoxious and all consuming. Fletcher is none of those things. Fletcher is weak, Fletcher is joyless, Fletcher is indecisive. Today I am not Fletcher. Today I am Jon.

"What's that you're reading?" she asks blankly.

The book I'm holding is a bit of smut I lifted from a hospital library. I tell her it's nothing, a work of fiction.

She asks why my arm is in a sling and I draw her a picture using pieces of truth mixed with things I've seen in movies to concoct a truly fantastic account of the day (in reality, Jon got miserably drunk, stole a bicycle, and crashed into a cement median).

We begin noticing each other's blatant fixations now. Hers on my mouth. Mine on her chest.

"Did they give you meds for the pain?" Says the poignant valley between her breasts.

I say, "Hydrocodone," and look up to her chin.

"MMMM," She licks her lips, "My fave."

Her eyes make an exaggerated change in focus toward the bus' bathroom door wedged between the rear bench seat and the engine. She gets up and walks over, looking back at me as she enters.

I hear the door shut behind her and then nothing. No latch. When I get up and turn down the galley to follow, I can see that I am right. The green color of vacancy resting precariously above the door's handle. I go to it.

She is sitting on the toilet with her knees pointing inward, her ankles cuffed together by white lace. She brings me to her and I shut the door. There is a violent crack as the green above the handle turns red. We strike a deal.

What happens inside is barbaric and unenthused. More of a routine necessity than anything else. We don't kiss. She is away from me and has no interest otherwise.

When we finish she doesn't move. Her back just straightens and the lace cuffs disappear under her faded yellow skirt. The part of each other we were interested in had already dripped out to the plastic floor beneath us.

I retrace my steps back to my seat. Several minutes pass before she comes back out. Paper, no doubt covered in an unrealized creation, goes whooshing down the toilet behind her.

The hair around the seams of her face is wet. I half expect her to throw a fit but instead, she just sits across from me, unfazed, reading some bogus magazine's political drivel.

I empty a few pills into my jacket pocket and toss her the bottle. It lands on the seat adjacent to hers. She keeps reading and the bottle disappears.

"Next stop," the driver calls over the bus's speaker system, "five minutes, Oxnard."

*Originally published as "Greyhound" in *Trenchfoot Gazette* in 2013

BANSHEE

Melanie was luminous and cherry-pie sweet. Impossibly blue eyes sought everything good in me. We surrounded ourselves with the convivial, spinning circuitously in our vicious little vortex like piss down a urinal. We laughed. We fought. For a while everything seemed, okay. Our minds found something useful in one another. But we were mutually parasitic. Just evil spawns of resentment drooling over the chance to rip our world to shreds and howl with delight as it feathers down over the remnants of a once shared heart.

Someone tells me "Karma is justice without the satisfaction," as I stare blankly into a bottomless glass. The piano keeps playing, napkin stacks grow tall and then thin out.

Just want to forget her. Just want to get her out of my fucking head. Can't breathe goddamnit. The bottle helps; it truly is the culprit for all things lost.

I finish another drink and (through the grace of irony) remember everything:

She was in the shower. I sat at my desk balking at a blank page. Empty bottles and cans and charred tobacco everywhere. I knew what was coming but pleaded with hope nonetheless. Her cell vibrated on the bed and the water turned off. The little screen taunted me and I was helpless. I took the chance and held my breath. The looming conclusion to a story I knew would be my last had fallen into my hands.

I can't wait to come home to you, mi amore.

I supposed it could have been out of context. A harmless flirtation fingering passed the edges of friend-ship, hoping to prove their world wasn't flat after all. But I knew I was willing myself a fool. When I opened the bathroom door she was coating a brush with pale powder. It was near midnight.

"Hey."

"Hi," she said between strokes.

"So I dunno' what our deal is but…"

"But what, Sean?"

Those blue eyes froze over as they found mine in the mirror.

"I don't think you're staying at Trisha's tonight."

The brush kept swaying.

"Why, 'cause I'm putting on makeup?"

"No," I said softly, "because her Facebook status says she's in the middle of a road trip." She passed me under the doorway wearing only a towel, then dressed behind our closet doors. The sight of her naked body was no longer my privilege.

"Why the fuck are you checking her Facebook?"

"You're going to see that guy."

She laughed. "You're such a stalker, you know that Sean? Total stalker."

"Look, I think it would be best for me and for you if you just told me."

"Told you what?" She said while angrily rummaging through her purse.

"Melanie, for real. Come on, I know you're seeing someone. That guy from work."

She stopped, then nervously bit her lip. The conversation had finally begun.

"I'm staying at his place, yea."

"So what, you're fucking this guy?"

"You know it's been shit with us," Melanie buttoned her jeans, found her keys in the dish by the door, "and I've been trying to have my own life. It's hard, but it's what I have to do. And yea, he and I go out for drinks and what not, and… I mean, what do you expect, you know?"

"And what, Mel?"

Her hand was resting on the door handle. She looked up and away, then down and back to me. The blue left her eyes and collected into little pools.

"And yes, we slept together."

I swallowed something terrible then. A heavy, beating stone filled my stomach. I knew it was coming and prepared myself for the worst. But I had no idea that I would feel so utterly embarrassed. It was the way she said it more than anything. "Slept together". So trite, so matter-of-fact, so cold.

She forgot to lock the door behind her, and I knew then for certain, it was the end of everything.

DOPEY

And as this all will inevitably end, so it shall begin, with me falling:

"No, no, NO!" I managed to scream in the most unattractive of pitches before slamming my knees, elbows, and chin into the pavement below. You see, at the same moment I noticed yet another of my favorite local shops was being forced to close, Charlie decided to use his massive English bulldog shoulders to drag me by the leash over to the bits of cheese and pepperoni floating in the gutter. Charlie went to slurping and I went to the ground.

It tasted salty and metallic; not the sidewalk or the vomit I thankfully missed, but the blood seeping through my teeth. All things considered, the tap on my chin was fairly soft but still strong enough for my molars to slice through part of my tongue.

"Get over here!" I shouted at Charlie, only in a lispy, swollen-tonguey, kind of way.

We sat there together for a moment, his big brown orbs staring up at me. We smiled together then, knowing the appropriateness of our dumb-luck. And he started to laugh. But not a deep, silly, Charlie laugh. It was a light, crisp, feminine sort of chuckle. His mouth stayed shut though, and I looked at him with the sort of cocked, quizzical head position that surely belonged to his kind.

"You two okay down there?" The voice said from somewhere above us, "Y'all look a little confused."

The sun was behind her and I couldn't get a good look at first. Her accent was distinctively southern but not at all overwhelmingly so. Probably Tennessee.

"Tyler," She said and held out her hand. I grabbed it and she leaned back and yanked with all her tiny frame could muster. Now back among the bipedal, I could get a better sense of who was speaking. Charlie did the same, his black-button nose at her feet.

She had emerald eyes and strawberry hair. Thin, delicate lips and tiny freckles that ran the length of her nose. She smelled sweet but not artificial. Like something familiar that you can't quite put your finger on but couldn't care less because it was even better not knowing.

We were still connected by the hands, "And you are?"

"Josh."

"And who's this young fella'?" She said, kneeling down pet my eager Bully.

"This is Charlie."

"Nice to meet you Charles," she rested her hands above and below his flapping jowls and looked back at me, "And you too, Joshua." Then she noticed my raw, red palms and the trickle of blood seeping through my lips, "Oh my god you're bleeding!"

She took the charcoal colored scarf off of her neck and wiped my face, then wrapped my hands. "You'll get an infection for sure," she said. And without pausing long enough for me to speak, she went on, "I'm going to be late back from lunch so I have to run. But I work in the big office building just up the street. You know it?" I nodded and she took out a pen and wrote B.P. Webber on the inside of my arm. "That's my boss. Come by whenever and you can return my scarf, preferably cleaned."

She smiled at me with wide eyes and shrugging shoulders, then turned away. Still unable to speak, all I could do was stare as she wiggled off. Charlie was just as star-struck by the whole thing. He just sat there with his legs off to one side and an open, panting jaw.

"I knew I loved you for *some* reason," I said to Charlie who just snorted and looked away, "C'mon buddy, it's gonna' be a good day."

*MADMAN

There's a pony keg of some German beer people never buy and it's covered with salted ice from the corner market but the beer still pours flat and heady. Everyone seems to be enjoying themselves over the sporadic fits of static interrupting a pop song coming from iPod speakers that I know I've heard before. And no one really cares because they're already too high or drunk to notice, even though the sun has yet to set on this second day of finals week.

I had just come from a luncheon with my mother where she unknowingly (maybe carelessly) accused me of being a "queen" who "can't handle responsibility" and has "eviscerated" the tidy sum entrusted to him by his late and irrelevant father; a man for whom nothing was ever good enough.

A pair of tattooed jocks in loafers laugh gently at what I can only assume is their own irony. One of the girls from the LGBT alliance with a shirt that says "those who trade liberty for safety deserve neither" makes a pass at a taut looking blonde I fucked sometime last term and I'm staring off the balcony into the Pacific ocean, trying to dump the ass-end of my lifeless German beer onto an ex-friend of mine who's hovering around the party below this one. And the speakers keep blaring this toxic-pop crap that I'm sure I should hate but can't stop my feet from tapping to.

"Peter?" She says from behind me, "Peter is that you?"

I turn, unsure of who is speaking even as I scan her face. I think her name is Kate.

"O-M-G, I can't believe it!" Maybe-Kate says and hugs me, her red cup drooling down my neck, "Where have you been all my life?" she asks, "wait…" and I have to because I can't think of anything to say, "tell me you're not back with Jenay," and she glares past me at a singeing red-headed girl I've never met, "are you?"

I choose not to respond at first and then, suddenly more sober than I'd like, tell her that I need a beer and that I'll grab one for her. She'll forget about it just as fast as I draw up and discard the memory of that weekend we spent together in Santa Barbara last June. The weekend we always woke up sweating, her hands cupping my flaccid cock, moaning softly, sorely, as I'd bite the small of her back.

"I have to pee," she chirps before receding into the crowd.

So I'm grabbing a brew from the keg when this guy Mike or Michael who I think I took Psychology of Women with offers me a joint and we smoke. My vision softens but somehow I remain incredibly focused on getting laid.

This girl Jenay that I'm supposedly fucking is splayed over the balcony puffing circles from a Parliament at the eaves. Her plain cotton camisole reaches up, exposing a refreshingly un-pierced navel, slightly damp. I imagine licking the sweat off of her, lapping at that soft, taut crevice until we're raw.

My beer's gone already. I grab another and my bladder is full. Bathroom's locked. I contemplate showering the door but it opens and my fly is down. Maybe-Kate steps through, pinching her ears and giggling in some awful pitch. Two red-eyed, snarling freshmen are behind her. One sitting on a toilet with a wall mirror on his lap, chopping little blue shards into segments, the other kneeling between his thighs, twisting a cracked bulb between her lips and blowing thick oily clouds.

"Hey, you," Maybe-Kate's head finds my shoulder, "Wanna' play with us?"

Guy-on-toilet introduces himself as "Jame-o" several times then continues his conversation with the mirror. The girl on her knees stares up at me stupidly, pulls me weakly to the floor and slips her sticky blue fingers into my mouth while coughing, then mumbles something like "sharing is caring" but I can't be sure. My gums are burning and I mouth to her "Yes please."

At first I don't know if I'm doing it right but then I feel it. I feel it. Fuck me, I can feel it. Then they're laughing and I am too. She tells me she's an art major and that The Beatles "suck balls". Jame-o asks me where I got my jacket, then looks despondently at the ceiling while humming. She drops her panties from under her skirt, white-lace cuffing her ankles. Jame-o's hand disappears and he's smiling at me. It sounds like she's getting off so I get up to leave and she asks me to stay but I apologize and go. The lock snaps behind me and I swear I can hear her choking through the door.

The crescent in the sky passes quickly. I'm sweating through the blazer I wish I wasn't wearing but underneath is what I woke up in: Black t-shirt, overpriced jeans, Converse no socks.

A girl smiles at me. It's getting hotter. There's a car out front filling with people that look motivated. I hop in and don't recognize anyone. Someone's touching my knees. The car-stereo is throbbing euro-junk but I'm laughing because I think we're headed downtown. Fifteen minutes and I'm spinning. Get off at a liquor store. Buy a warm quart of beer because the fridges are broken and the cars gone. Ask a stranger for the nearest bar. A trucker drops me off at a bar called "Creekside". There really is a creek. Smells strange but I stay for drinks. Pink shooters and vodka-sodas and something green and on fire. I throw up in my seat, or on the bar, or in my mouth and swallow. The tender calls me a cab, asks where, and I don't remember falling asleep.

When I wake up, she's already screaming. How I convinced her to come home with me is a mystery. What's clear is that my sheets are cold and dank and sticky in such a familiar way that I know immediately I have pissed myself.

She makes for a quick exit, jeans unbuttoned, blouse at her waist, growling at her shoes or herself or the door for slowing her down.

Trying to sound apologetic I tell her, "Good stuff."

"Fuck off," she says.

I shrug, she feebly mimics, and leaves.

The sun is yet to rise but I can already feel it and I'm crazy hungry. The apartment is riddled with empty, broken things from nights less interesting than you'd think. My briefs are stuck to me and I'm still wearing a condom but it's ripped down the middle and I can't remember if it happened during or after. What

I do remember is the weight of her hips against my chin, blonde hair and the taste of almonds.

*Originally published as "Honesty From a Pathological Liar by *Crossed Out Magazine* 2012

*KINDRED SPIRITS

I get most of my sleep at strip clubs. Where else can you find complete darkness during the lightest part of the day? A monotonous darkness. A deep, melodic beating. A soothing hum swaying me to sleep.

I like to sit in the farthest corner from the stage after tipping the bartender one-hundred percent on my two required beverages. That usually keeps them from complaining. Only once in a great while when I stay asleep longer than a few hours do they ask me to leave.

I remember one such incident when I hadn't sept for over two days. I was in a dry area of California where strip clubs were few and far between. When I finally found one, the sun had set and I was a mess. I could barely talk. I don't know how long I spent at the bar before I passed out.

I woke up outside, surrounded by cinder blocks

and bocce balls.

I was in the backyard of some college kids' rental home. Their blaring T.V. woke me from the sand. When I got up to walk towards the noise I found a girl sitting on a make-shift bench, playing on her computer and drinking champagne from the bottle. Two dogs sat at her feet, slowly waging their tails and yawning. I asked her for the time.

"Six." She said.

The sun's positioning was inconclusive, "In the morning?"

She nodded, covered her ears with headphones that trailed to her laptop and lifted the bottle to her lips before holding out an offering.

We spent the next few hours on the bench passing the bottle between us while skipping through a documentary called *Losing the Messiah*. At one point she turned to me and said, "Every time I see that intervention show, I realize that I'm not trying hard enough to be an addict."

"I couldn't agree more," I said between mouthfuls.

"I'm just not good at it I guess. But I *am* trying so that counts, right? I mean, there must be a difference between not being good at something and being bad at something."

She didn't seem interested in much of a response,

so I kept quiet. She was pretty—not perfect. One of those almost-everywhere, not-quite-anywhere type of girls. She had a boyish figure like someone who hadn't quite grown into themselves yet. Her arms were lanky and her hair was a tangled mess. She had freshly popped pimples on her chin and some older ones around her hairline. But her eyes were sweet and just bright enough to command your attention away from any and all blemishes.

"What was your name again doll?" She asked politely as if we had met once before at some long forgotten party.

"Fletcher, you?"

"Jenny."

She bounced as she said her name and something about it just killed me. Something about the auspicious nature of her youth. Her flagrant, unprotected world devoid of consequence. She was at the beginning of something I'd long since forgotten. And I think I fell in love with her that day. With champagne, puppy dogs, Jenny, and bocce balls all at six in the morning.

*Originally published as "Bocce Balls" by *Crossed Out Magazine* 2014

*RUNNER RUNNER

One

We may be enamored by love stories, but intrigue lays in the tragic. Unfortunately, the space between is too small for things like memory and empathy and people who give a shit to find a place, though just wide enough to harbor a collaborative of everything irritating.

Like most things formulaic, her argument begins: blah blah blah you don't listen, why is it that this and that make you do the opposite, I don't know why I put up with you...

Her monotone continues as I stare off and up. Leaves hang above our words like little pieces of time, fragments of before in the image of after, hoping for happily and ever.

She accepts my brooding silence as some sort of

"well-deserved" apology, then kisses me sweetly above the brow and scampers off through the kitchen to the bed of pillows sprawled purposefully across the wooden floor. A flickering box distanced by mere inches blankets her pallor in a monastic glow. She tears at her thumbs and affixes herself to the inane drivel spewing forth.

I am diaphanous to her. A fourth wall. She sees, hears, and thinks as she pleases, discarding the rest as inconsequential. Unimportant. Dead to her.

Once upon a time she had a discernible shape. Cheek bones, ankles, a waist. Nothing more than a waif hovering gently above the eggshells. But this loose mound lounging clumsily before me has long since consumed her.

A certainty: I remain remorseless either way. For I am but a "twenty-something nobody" with "nothing anyone would be interested in" she often explains to me. And I have tried all forms of the convivial—save for getting laid—to suppress the pageant of oddities matriculating between my ears, yet, it continues in spite.

Sarah (in case you were wondering her name) is the abysmal woman—teetering on the floor, watching E true Hollywood stories—that I am misfortunate enough to be engaged to. Although you wouldn't know it by the sight of her left hand as the ring had become a permanent fixture in the soap dish by the sink nearly two years ago. It probably wouldn't fit that fan of sausages she calls fingers anymore anyway.

"Are you cooking something in there Chris?" she asks, as if the distant thought of minced meat encased in entrails had telepathically triggered her flapping jowls.

"No dear," I manage to squeak back.

I don't blame her really. It's not entirely her fault. I had been mentally absent far longer than the visibility of her bone structure had. And to be fair, I am nothing to be proud of either: I've been in an out of jobs for the past two years (more often out than in), I drink heavily and in secret as to avoid the belittlement that launched this impossibly circuitous habit in the first place. I've gained weight, I've lost ambition, I am irascible and cold and wildly speculative. I am someone I never wanted to be, but am, and loathe.

At least I *tried* to love her, I truly did, but somewhere between the giggles of our youth and the wrought-iron grimaces carried today, we lost each other. We lost ourselves.

We once had dreams and ambition and interesting things to say. People listened. People cared. But that has passed. And so I have decided on this hot August night, that a change is necessary, a drastic, volcanic change.

I must escape. Escape to all the fucks, snorts, and swallows that I should have already been bored with by now. To be able to move, run, live, and create. To be the someone and do the something that I've always known I am capable of.

"I'm going out," I say to that full volume static that all too often follows my voice, "I'm going out I said!"

A beat goes by, then another, and my keys lay limply in the door behind me.

Two

The best part of a downward spiral is the beginning. Before all the self-loathing reaches full strength and keeps you from turning on lights or going outside. You give up small things at first, bathing, eating right, brushing your teeth. Then you start to replace everything good in your life with the worst things possible. Self-destruct mode I believe it's called. And when it finally became my turn to escape this vicious cycle, chance would have me on a southbound, California train:

Summer showers come with the night and as the water cracks against the window I almost feel comfortable. But rain lies. It promises a fresh start, new beginnings, cleanliness. Yet pools turn brown and muddy and grey to match the lackluster above. The train picks up speed and darkness overwhelms us with a strange humidity—an uneasy warmth—and here I sit inside, well sheltered, but somehow still colder than the inches filling under me.

I just wish I had given myself more of a chance, more credit for just being me, instead of rushing, rushing, rushing, to an ending that wasn't all that great. With Sarah, I became someone I never wanted to be. Someone undefined.

Personally, I consider ambiguity to be among the most frightening aspects of life. Like all those horrifying propositions that include the word "someday". Someday it will happen, someday my promises will be kept, someday I'll die. But I feel different about it now. Because as I pass through this world, holding fast behind thick and hazy glass, I am reminded of how beautiful it can be. And I cannot help but smile because "someday" has finally come.

"Union Station, ten minutes." An omnipresent voice updates. Ten minutes from an escape, ten minutes until freedom. Ten minutes to forget *all* this.

My cell-phone rings, it's Sarah. A picture of her posing the way young girls do for prom photos comes up on my cell-phone's screen. I feel sick and hastily find my way to the restroom in the café car on the bottom level.

It's occupied. I ignore the call.

Music plays delicately over the café car speakers. Music that's older than I am, that shouldn't bring back any memory of anything but demands it of me regardless. Inviting me to empathize with loves I haven't lost and laughs I haven't had. When newer songs come on—though they are still old to me—I want to weep. Weep because I don't remember them the way I thought I did. Because the only memories that have yet to escape me are the blurred and the meaningless.

A teenager blowing smoke out of a cracked window looks at me and laughs at my listlessness. I imagine an impulse: charging him against the wall and squeezing what little life there could possibly be from his young, slender throat.

My phone rings again, that picture returns and I march to him furiously.

"Hey, hey, wait a minute dude, I didn't mean any…"

I stop him with a defeated smile and revise my intention, "Spare a smoke?"

Confused but interested, the kid tells me it's his last one and offers a drag instead.

The last time I had a cigarette is beyond my memory, which makes me sad, but then the nicotine settles in. Dilated veins inflate an insolent brain. I am light. The glimpse of relief has me delirious and I fumble the cigarette to the floor. The kid twists it out with his toes and disappears up the staircase. Cool tendrils of wind sneak through the glass and singe my cheeks. My fingers smell of figs. I think I'm happy.

Again, my phone, that picture. Everything stops. My grip is immense. I want to crush it like one of those little origami cranes people make. Completely vulnerable to me. Controlled.

The woman I once loved—hand on hip, shoulders back—goes flying into the darkness and onto the tracks. Best left to the inland empire from whence it came.

The voice again, "Now arriving, Union station."

She'll never find me.

Three

"Welcome to Los Angeles International Airport," the programmed attendant offers, "How may I assist you?"

"I know this sounds odd," I say, "but I'm looking for the next flight out. Farthest I can get from here," I pause then add, "Without leaving California."

Throwing a dart at a map never seemed less cliché.

"Sir?" She stares blankly.

"Anywhere, random. I don't really care. The far-thest I can get from here on-the-cheap."

I wink.

Without blinking she begins to type.

"Just yourself?"

Yes.

"Any baggage?"

No.

More typing.

"I have a flight to San Diego leaving at 5pm and one to San Francisco at 3," she says abruptly.

Embarrassed, I ask the time. She tells me it's noon.

"Diego or Francisco, huh." A lengthy pause puts my coherency in question, receiving a cool, furled lip.

Unwilling to accept infringement on efficiency, she interrupts, "or I can have you in Dallas, Denver, Detroit…"

I stop her recitation midway and take a chance, "Where would *you* choose?"

She looks up from her monitor, sees my expressionless face and shifts her weight from one hip to the other: She's an average looking blonde, maybe thirty, pale eyes and thin lips, ample breasts that all but bore holes through her blouse (were they not obscured by a graying blue blazer and a tie befitting a birthday present more than a collar).

"I really wouldn't know, Sir."

Fleeting patience sifts through my pockets for a coin we make a wager, "Heads, S.F. Tails, S.D." The coin spins effortlessly through the air. I want to catch it, but don't. Four, five, six bounces and a President's face smiles up at us.

Her eyebrows raise and wait for confirmation. I nod.

More typing ensues, more questions are asked, various plastic placards are presented, then disappear. And after an invasive trip through the security laden mezzanine, all I have to do is wait.

Four

If you have never found yourself in the middle of a crowded food court, guiltily devouring a cinnamon or cheese coated whatever, sipping on a three dollar beer you paid eight for, then you have never been in love at LAX. But I'm in no mood for saturated treats and with half-an-hour to kill plus a mounting head-ache, I find myself at one of the many airport bars; a six stool walk-up devoid of patrons, save for myself and another man about my age.

He wears thin glasses and a slightly off center baseball cap with a team logo I don't recognize. His blonde hair makes a speckled trail down his cheeks and gradually forms patches as it circles his mouth.

"You chief bro?" he says to me in a strange mix-ture of southern drawl and surfer-speak.

"I'm sorry?"

"Chief bro. You chief?"

Without understanding, (and wanting to avoid yet another uncomfortable hesitation) I quickly respond, "Yea man, sure."

He searches through his bag and comes out with a sloppy looking granola bar that he claims to have made, well, "special".

"'Triple-Berry Chocolate'," he calls them, "Even though there are actually four berries, I think 'Triple-Berry' sounds better." He lists the berries and elaborates, "Plus two types of raisins. And sesame seeds!"

Then he splits the seedy treat in half and we eat. I order a drink and he finishes his. He tells me his name is Joshua and that he owns a skate-shop in Santa Barbara. Recently divorced, he decided to take a vacation. My curiosity can't help but prod him for an explanation.

"Well, funny story," he laughs, "Got me on the credit card bills."

"Funky charges or something?"

"Nah, that's the thing. Never use a card when I'm 'doin' my *thing*'. Knew she'd check."

"Then, what was it?"

"See, she's goin' down the line items and comes across this eighty-some-odd-dollar charge from a place called 'Great Legs'. Being the cynical bitch that she is, she assumes that I had been visiting a brothel that's stupid enough to take credit cards," Josh looks to the bartender, points at his empty glass, then himself, a drink comes quickly and he takes a pull, then continues, "So I come home one night, she's furious. Throwing shit around and screaming. The whole deal. *My* dumb ass thinks that she found some panties or went through my emails or whatever those crazy housewives on T.V. do, and I panic, figure she knows everything, and decide to come clean."

Not knowing what to say, I make a defeated face.

"Yea, the bitch'll never speak to me again. Shouldn't of done it, I know, but fuckit, one life to live you know?" Josh closes his eyes and takes a heavy pull on the drink, finishing it.

"So, what was the funny part of all this?" I finally ask.

A laugh escapes his nose.

"'Great Legs' is a winery."

We drift off then, the triple berry high lurching ever closer to the incomprehensible. A soft burning creeps in. My focus has its own pulse. We sit awhile and watch as people pass us by. Us so stationary, them so animated yet still in slower motion than normal. Reunions of old friends, returning family, lovers together once again. The smiles their faces make, the undeniable warmth they give to one another. Eyes light up like fairytale truths to a single recognizant face among the crowd, looking past to a familiar world beyond the taxi lined curb.

Josh is gone. The bartender changes shifts. My plane is boarding and I get a prickling feeling behind my ears.

*Originally published as "Hopeful For Never" by *eFiction Publishing 2013*

THE ALPHA

Famed Therapist Dead at 55, a local paper prints. The LGBT Alliance posts a blurb on its site *Insidious Dr. B.P. Webber Finally Gets His. Esquire* and *Maxim* co-sponsor a slapdash biopic titled something like *Losing the Messiah.* Dr. Webber spent his life counseling broken marriages, despondent young couples, damaged men and women desperate to be the person that true love can't help but embrace. "Herein," he'd often tell his patients, (or "students" as he saw it) "lies your fundamental problem."

None of those once enraptured souls would attend his funeral as they'd most likely obey his first rule of inter-relational success "Emotional reaction is dispersed in the mind not in the body". He purported that such reactions as remorse, guilt, and psychological attachment make up the foundation for the poison that is codependency.

This Dr. B.P. Webber, a couples therapist buried deep in the void where Orange County's heart might have been, was made famous by his unique system of restoring relationships to success by "stealthily instituting biologically predisposed behavioral patterns to reestablish a functionally interdependent hierarchy of intimacy" or rather, he believed that relationships suffer from what he theorized was a simple, calculable, affliction: Women are attracted to the "Alpha-Male" and the qualities that lay therein. Driven to secure a man with Passion, determination, and confidence, quintessential masculinity, etc. However, once such an Alpha is identified and obtained, a circuitous dichotomy arises shortly thereafter. Subconsciously the female will mill their Alpha through a set of trials(or what Dr. Webber would call "mothering") meant to instill dependency. This psychological melee is an effort to obscure her Alpha from primal competition by making him appear entirely contrary: A psychological state described in, and sharing a title with, the Dr.'s bestselling book, "Betatized". A concept which, after its publication, would be referenced often and rather glibly, by a large part of the male community?.

This of course caused a stir among the waterfront community in which we lived. Newport Beach, California's plastic-gold crown, perforated by palm trees and sushi spots and yachts with taut masts. It garnered praise as well as distain. Some spat his name; others spoke of divinity.

He did help people as far as providing a service that was wanted, delivering exactly as he had promised, that sort of thing. This much I've seen with my own eyes. As his assistant for the past 15 years I've seen miserable pairs emerge from his office gleaming with confidence. I've seen downtrodden introverts come back with wife and children in tow, just to shake his hand in gratitude. I've seen diamond rings double in karats. A grandfather remarry. A once virgin approaching thirty regularly leaves him voicemail updates regarding his nearly completed quest to "finish" the karma sutra. Dr. B.P. Webber was effective, there's no disputing that. But his methodology was questionable to the audience at large. They called him guru and expert, even genius just as often as misogynist and "bitter old quack". Or as one headline put it, "Devious Dr. Webber, DEAD. Lesser spiders report increased business."

SILICON MAN

It's "Cougar Night" at *The Rose*. He's on the balcony three floors up, the Olympic-sized pool staring back at him. Highballs and cocktails and cigars float by effortlessly. It's all Prada and Gucci and Louis Vuitton. A jazz trio plays softly somewhere as waitresses click through the crowd on their little brown heels, in their little brown dresses, with little brown trays.

"Good crowd tonight," A black suit and tie says to him and lights a long thin cigarette, "Wouldn't you say?"

He smiles respectfully, presses some air through dry nostrils and retrains on the pool below. The suit finishes its cigarette and disappears.

His clasped hands twitch against each other in an awkward rhythm. Coming on all of a sudden then not at all. His eyes are black, totally dilated as the green light reflecting from the pool's basin screams up at him. From a distance you might think him at peace, standing there in the luminescent glow of *The Rose* and its unbridled opulence. He's at the top of everything, yet he feels leagues below it all.

"Mark," a gentle voice caresses his back, "Mark honey, they're ready for us."

He turns knowingly with a well-practiced smile and grabs her by the waist. Luxurious black hair reaching delicate shoulders. Deep bronze skin, full crimson lips that never quite come together, impossibly blue eyes made all the more glorious under the full California moon.

Her name is Andrea. A well-bred beauty all the way from Bombay India. Her family brought with them an already ample wealth that multiplied many times over since their arrival in the States. Her father a brilliant electrical engineer turned entrepreneur, her mother an American born to a family of medical doctors involved in pharmaceutical miracles.

"I love you, you know." He says, pulling her closer.

"I know," and she kisses him sweetly, wipes the touch of lipstick from his mouth, "Come on, birthday-boy."

She takes his arm and they saunter back into the lounge where a tall, French, waiter will guide them to a waiting feast. A large round table stuffed with eyes and noses and mouths he couldn't care less about. A room filling with judgment and betrayal just minutes before a merciless clock strikes midnight and ages him to thirty years.

And as they make their way, he takes a last look at all he has accomplished. The pool, the lights, the dress, the glass, the pride and glory and the love under his arm. One last look at everything he is about to lose.

KIND-OF HEART

Darling,

I am writing you this because I love you and because I am really concerned about you right now. Recently you have really upset me, not so much with your actions, but with your arguments and justifications for your actions. I think that you don't fully understand how irrational you can be when you drink. When you apologized you didn't mention anything you did or said, it was just general. Is that because you don't remember? Or did you really think that a vague apology was going to make it ok to act so irrational?

Notice I'm not saying that you are crazy because I don't think that you are crazy. However, you do act completely illogical and foolish after you drink.

You have acted like this far too often for it to be excused anymore. I really have never gotten upset with you but this has gone too far. When did you start hating everyone? For the first time in our relationship I am completely hurt by you.

I know that you care, I know you do. If you are trying to get attention, you are going about it all wrong. You are a completely different person when you drink. You yell and fight with anyone in your path and then say rude thing after rude thing thus alienating yourself. Then you sober up and justify your actions to make it seem ok in your mind when in reality it is not. And we are still mad.

It's not fair for anyone to take your verbal abuse. I wouldn't wish that on you and I don't understand why you do it to me. It's not ok anymore. What I first thought was just a phase has clearly turned out to not be. I have watched you fall for too long.

I really think you need to get help and stop drinking. Your drinking is interfering with your life and I don't think that you are a particularly happy person anymore. You can't deny that you have done a lot of stupid shit because of the amount you drink. I haven't seen you as a happy drunk in almost a year. Once you have a few drinks in you, your personality changes, and no longer for the better. Being called a "filthy cunt" for taking your car keys away after you drank an entire bottle of vodka is just one example that is forever scarred in my mind.

I don't know how else to tell you how I feel other

than writing you this letter because when I try to talk to you about it, you interrupt and fight me. I'm tired of being your cheerleader and trying to convince myself that you will come around. You have shown me that you have a serious problem that needs to be addressed.

You are losing your friends. I know that deep down that bothers you. If you keep acting the way you do and drink the way you do, I will have no other choice than to remove myself from your life.

I really do love you and have had so many great times with you. Going to the zoo, eating at that little Greek café, Sushi nights; the memories are all wonderful.

I hope that you take this to heart and take this seriously. Your drinking is hurting us. I've tried to get through to you for the last time. Please get help. Get happy again. Get your life back. You don't have to live like this if you don't want to.

If you are sober reading this, can you see why I am at my wits end?

I miss you and I just want the old you back.

-    Love, Mel.

MY DISSIDENT NARCISSIST

We were doomed from the start but I never could have predicted the way it would finally end. Jenny was a lush and had no idea how or when to stop anything once she started. We went to a restaurant uptown for a company party hosted by the business she worked for. It was a nice enough place. The bar was made of black granite with rounded wooden edging. The shelves behind it were lit by dim blue and red lights that reflected back and forth between the bottles and the mirror behind it. There was a large dance floor that was obviously decorated on an office staff budget and by an office staff member. Beyond the dance area was an empty DJ booth next to double doors leading to an outdoor patio; complete with fire pit and ash trays. An adult playground where people convene to share belligerence.

After about twenty minutes the place was packed.

Five minutes later, Jenny was nowhere to be found. No doubt dancing as sexually as possible with as many men as she could find. Instead of trying to find her and becoming irate at the site of her promiscuity (like she would have loved me to do), I sat down at the bar and switched from beer to double vodka-sodas. I drank the first one, delicious, I drank a second, divine, I drank a third, and I was hungry. There was catered food out on the patio. Once my plate was properly mounded with everything I could possibly fit, I looked for a seat. I found a bench near the edge of the patio that was unoccupied and made a bee line for it. I probably got three spoonful's into my mouth before Jenny's "He's enjoying himself too much" alarm went off and she went searching for me.

Her bright blonde hair materialized instantly in front of me. She slapped the paper plate of food out of my lap and replaced it with her rear looking at me with one eye squinted and the other aimed at my chin in a way I am sure she thought looked sexy.

With her arms around my neck she pulled my ear to her lips and nibbled as her wet mouth gargled out "You have to take me home and fuck me, right now".

I now loved her almost as much as I hated her.

As expected, I galloped and she stumbled towards the front of the restaurant to begin our walk home. She seemed way too drunk for the amount of time we spent there, but then again, so did I. The restaurant was only a ten minute walk from my home so I did my best to drag her along. I carried her into the house over my shoulder with her tiny dress barely covering her panties. I shuffled to my room as quickly as possible and threw the useless sack of tequila she had become onto my bed. I slid off her black pumps and set them by the bed so she wouldn't go ape-shit in the morning trying to find them. My dark red sheets were furled underneath her so I wrapped her up as best I could with my comforter and surrounded her head with pillows. She looked like an idiot, and that's how I wanted her to feel when she woke up.

I closed my bedroom door and entered the kitchen to make myself another vodka-soda. Then another and another. After a while I ran out of club soda and just started pouring vodka on the rocks with a twist of lime–not a good choice. When I became confused enough that I forgot where the floor ended and my legs began, I crawled my way back to the bedroom to curl up with my drunken counterpart. She had thrown all of the pillows off of the bed in her sleep and pulled the comforter so tightly around her upper body that her bottom half lay bare exposing what must have truly inspired the shape of candy hearts. I slid my arms under her to move her far enough over that there would be room for me. But when my hands glided between her waist and the sheets I felt something wet. Something soaked. I yanked my hands out from under her in disbelief.

"I can't be this drunk." I said to myself. I lifted my hands up to my nose and recognized the smell immediately.

She had pissed herself. But she never gave much of a shit about anything she did wrong, so why would this be any different. It made no difference to either of us at that point anyway.

*KISSLESS AND CARELESS

The sun over this tar infested water is so bright that I can only dream of a gloomy day to deaden the noise. It's not that I am depressed, or even have a reason to be. All I see is blonde after blonde running along the beach with a margarita in one hand, a wad of cash in the other, and legs that never quite seem to come together. Maybe it's my bi-polarity surfacing, but this image alone makes me want to slam my head against the wall just to make sure I can still feel something.

I live in a dream world that allows for anything to happen. Giving out countless opportunities to fulfill whatever conquests one could invent. A lifestyle that is easily managed due to its complete subsidization. Yet, I can't for the life of me find one person who can manage it.

The biggest concern for most of my peers is how they are going to afford the exorbitantly expensive nights downtown while maintaining a steady drug addiction, without being forced to secure a job. Most of the people I associate with either cannot hold a respectable occupation for more than a week because the great pay and minimal hours were "too demanding" or they have never worked a day in their life due to a trust-fund or trust-fund-equivalent. It is really quite an astonishing talent to be able to mumble-fuck your rational thought process so well that you actually believe you can survive this way.

Truth be told, I am just jealous. Jealous of biologically predisposed ignorance, and sun-kissed bodies, and those that sit in front of a video game while eating an oven-bake pizza, wondering where the day has gone. But I should admit that I have found myself succumbing to these vices as well. The alluring Pacific coast with its perfectly arranged palms, and beach bar after beach bar that keep beckoning me closer with promises of drunken encounters and temporary amnesia. Of course the resulting hours spent in the shower when you wake from your coma, in an attempt to scrub the whatever disease you're convinced you've contracted off of your genitals is not quite as glamorous as the impetus.

What I want to know is what monumental change occurred to alter everyone's perception of integrity, respect, and more importantly, innocence. I know that's as cliché as it gets but bear with me.

It seems that we have so adamantly insisted upon destroying the auspicious experience that is our youth. It is as if we forgo our innocence at an early age and replace it with private pre-schools, hapless tutors, and yoga classes. Then this army of American Idol contestants is expected to rediscover their innocence during adulthood, which of course manifests itself in the variety of ways referenced in the aforementioned.

And just as pessimism tightened the last loop of rope around my neck because a six year old somewhere in Eurasia beat me at online chess, I found what I was looking for.

I would tell you what her hair looked like but I don't think that brilliance is a color. Her eyes were brown though, chestnut brown, with that kind of wide open, misty glaze that leaves you wanting more. I could tell immediately that she was eager to please, selfless, and more loving than I could ever hope to be. She was delicate and reserved, with a smile that impaled me and a laugh that rang in my ears for days at a time.

I couldn't ask for more, especially considering I usually shot for much less. Not to say that my standards are infinitesimal, it is just a testament to how staggeringly perfect this girl, woman, was in every single way. Her name was Elle. And she turned out to be the missing spark that prevented me from ever really getting started.

Unfortunately she hated me. In fact, that doesn't quite emphasize her absolute loathing of me and everything about me as much as abhorrence does. I was a self-involved, arrogant, prick with all the vanity and naivety of the peers that I berate.

We were opposites, and still I wanted her from the moment we first met. Elle and I worked together at one of those retail fashion companies that proposes all women should be paper thin, and that the sluttier you are the better. My name was written all over it, hers wasn't. Unfortunately for Elle, I have this terrible habit of being able to hold an in-depth conversation while maintaining eye contact and then actually retaining the information that is spoken to me. Most girls call this affliction a "good listener". I prefer to regard it as patience combined with an ability to multi-task.

Each day I would surreptitiously design my lunch schedule to coincide with hers in hopes of casually crossing paths and "spontaneously" arrange an informal date, which after weeks of calculation, eventually was set for a Friday. We went to a bowling alley (something she decided) with a gay couple (also her decision) she was friends with. Definitely not in my top ten choices of how to initiate our romance but I like to think I am versatile enough to adapt to any situation. She wore black, I wore blue. And until I have a few drinks that's pretty much all I can remember about most people anyway.

As I sat at the bar waiting for my quintessential light-beer and some neon drink for Elle that was sure to cause a sugar induced seizure, I got an overwhelming feeling of disgust. I looked around where I was seated and became suddenly aware of the horrifying amount of consumption going on. Deep fried everything (shovel sold separately), booze of all sorts, clothing labels flashing under the chintzy disco lighting, cigarette smoke billowing in from the exits, and innumerable drugs behind everyone's eyes.

I finished choking on a bit of my own vomit, then turned to the gentleman/bum next to me who had a perplexed look on his face as if utterly confused over how the twelve empties in front of him learned to talk. I wanted to slap him across the face. I wanted to slap everyone across the face and scream "STOP! Is total inebriation your only means of subsistence? Are we all so deadened by pain that we have to mentally check out just to feel comfortable with each other?" It was just about then I received my two gargantuan beverages and signed the bill, "Hypocrite".

By the time I looked up from the bar to search the crowd for those allusive brown eyes, she was already next to me.

"Where are your friend's" I asked in a defeated sort of way.

She paused, searching my face for something. I

swear women are born with a disturbing ability to read a man's emotions through his facial expressions no matter how discrete or disguised they may be. She grabbed me by the hand and marched me out to the parking lot. It was strangely crisp out, especially for a summer night. We approached an isolated car and Elle spun around, her back arched, nestling itself along the car's silhouette. In one motion she grabbed me by the collar and pulled my lips close to, but just out of reach of, hers. The cold air made her breath visible as it surrounded my cheeks and floated off. Her nose fit perfectly alongside mine as she nuzzled each side, careful to just breeze by with her lips. I can't recall a time where I was ever so fixated. We stood there frozen, the rest of it all drawing back far away from us; two 20-somethings in the late night mist, pressed against each other, apprehensive, in expectation of a connection, a feeling, those shooting stars and fireworks our grandparents told us about but never believed was more than a fairytale. It was my move and I knew it. But for some reason, I couldn't.

Every part of my being wanted to, but something in me shut off. I felt like a kid on a playground that didn't understand anything more about life than how to swing to the next monkey bar. No knowledge of break-ups, or cheating, or lies, or tears, or loss. Just kissless and careless. It was as if I was unable to comprehend how a girl, woman, like Elle could ever be interested in someone like me.

In retrospect, I think my hesitation was because I realized in that tender moment under the fog of our knotted breaths, that this was something special. Someone who I wanted to be with for the long run. And it couldn't be won with pride or fury but patience.

The fumbled make-out session was just the beginning for Elle and me. Three weeks' worth of dates went by before we slept together. Sex is a necessary complication that changes the parameters of a relationship drastically. Although for the most part I find that if you really care about your partner unconditionally, then even the worst lay can be tolerated. We have an uncanny ability to purposefully deny the existence of a multitude of annoyances in an attempt to maintain our perception of happiness.

Interjectionally, there is something to be said for a woman who knows how to saddle up and take an active role in the bedroom. More bluntly, there is something fundamentally wrong with a woman who will only *be* fucked. I drifted off into this ponderous world of degeneracy during a managerial accounting class I was taking at city college. I must have made some sort of hung over transition from "direct labor standards" to "sexual labor standards" just before I collapsed on my desk and burped up a partial fish taco. Regardless of the state of mind, there is no way of emulating the feeling of two bodies moving, flowing even, in one repetitious motion. The intense emotional connection that finds new rhythms with each heart beat and gentle moan, every drip of sweat, and the sound of dry mouths painfully trying to swallow, desperate for release.

Regardless, Elle was perfect for me. She was much smarter than me, opinionated, unafraid to challenge, sophisticated, domesticated, other words that end in *-ated*. During sex she came, but not always. She had an insatiable appetite for discovery and wasn't apprehensive about getting her hands dirty. She could drink as much as me and still talk the cops out of giving me a citation for public intoxication. All of my friends were her friends and all of her friends were my friends. The only thing standing in our way was my crippling lack of true confidence.

This deficiency in confidence is ironically masked by an over exhibition of arrogance that shares a likeness to the head of a penis peering over the steering wheel of its red, Porsche convertible. It is an unwavering curse that's magnitude can only be paralleled by my pessimism. Unfortunately, I have found that this affliction is incurable and that the only escape is to live through other people's vitality and unquenchable thirst for life. If only I were strong enough to be my boring self: I'd give anything to be away from this madness, passed out under a palm tree with a corona in one hand and a wedding ring on the other. Maybe it's the hopeless romantic in me, or maybe I'm just hopeless.

Elle didn't seem to think so. She had confidence in me; she had enough confidence for the both of us. She was the perfect host for my parasitic obsession with need. I wanted people to commit to me without being committed to them. I required someone to be completely infatuated with me so that I wouldn't be fearful of losing them, and I needed to appear detached so that when they did eventually abandon me I wouldn't feel so desolate. This structured defense mechanism is most likely derived from my early perceptions of commitment through my parents' tattered examples.

If my parents were ever in love it was before I was born. As a child, I lived in constant fear of them separating and grew to become a mediator—a crutch really—to their crumbling relationship. I learned how to tranquilize people's anger and read their emotions through minute facial expressions and body language. It was the only way I could keep things together. I don't blame them though, I can't blame them. They gave me everything I ever wanted and at the same time taught me never to expect anything.

Keeping a relationship alive is an arduous task. It is draining, time consuming and never seems to give back quite what you put into it. Like a small child it must be steadily nurtured without an understanding of why.

Even with Elle, I remained skeptical to the idea that love had finally accepted me into its grasp. I was always looking for the exits in case love decided to turn on me.

But how could Elle love someone like that? She was so forbearing to our world. I can only assume that she either enjoyed my pessimism as a "yin" to her "yang" or that she was merciful enough to overlook my pettiness. It was of little concern to me as my head was always on a treasure hunt up my ass whenever she tried to help me work through such shortcomings.

Somehow, our lust continued within love's embrace. As frustrated as I would get with my inability to change the world around me, I knew I had her to keep me grounded. Being able to melt away in her warmth at will. Sleeping in and lazing around in the summer heat, unwilling to wear anything but each other's sweat.

I was so content I didn't know whether to laugh or cry. Maybe both. It was all new to me, for I had never experienced real love before.

In the past I had professed my love to numerous women (while in the midst of removing their bra or— preferably—panties) but this was a horse of a different color. We could lay in bed talking all afternoon with only short interruptions for tender sessions of kissing. We could tell each other anything and know that it would remain between us. I was finally able to trust someone; I was finally able to rest.

The summer was coming to a close and I was excited about the future. Elle and I became inseparable. At work, at school, at home, at parties, everything had new meaning. I woke up each day feeling energized and excited to fulfill my daily obligations. Finally motivated to keep living since my true purpose had been found.

Indeed, having all my bodily fluids drained night after night most likely played an integral role in my enlightenment, but that's beside the point. My perspectives had changed. I found myself thinking about marriage, even children. Now, I just had to figure out how and when my manic-depressive, lack-of-confidence, pessimistic tendencies were going to resurface and slit this relationship's jugular. I had to figure out a way to keep it together this time. I couldn't lose her, not after all this. I needed to solidify the commitment and make sure that my craziness was tucked safely away somewhere.

I quit drinking and she moved in just before Fall.

*Originally published in part as "Tarballs" in *Making Waves* 2011

*ENCHANTED

She left vodka and scrambled eggs for me on the nightstand. I won't eat them. We are in those tentative hours where today and tomorrow are irrelevant. There is orange juice and a cloudy glass. I mix things and drink them. It doesn't seem to help. I don't know what to do with myself and so, instead of finding sleep, I pine, concupiscent for her.

The house (more of a manor really) died long ago. The smell of it, the feel of it, the noise: dead, dead, dead. I'm in a guest room that once upon a time acted as a living quarters for a maid or nanny or slave. Getting up three or four times without success I can only dream of reaching for the door.

The staircase beyond, lugubrious and daunting, seems an impossible feat. But I know that somewhere above me she lay angelic and sleepless, a wandering hand leaving gentle kisses across her neck.

I can hear her restlessness and begin to wonder: Shall I ascend these great depths to the forbidden? Do I possess the benevolent steps necessary to traverse such an illicit path?

And I am halted. Annoyed, frightened, and... halted: Her father sleeps noisily and alone beside my proffered boarding. Through the vents I hear him. Tossing, turning, groaning at the restless night. I remove my covers valiantly, somehow willing myself to take a step. The pine squeaks. He grumbles something about lost monies and turns over, content with what is unbeknownst. Another step; I can feel his beating heart though I cannot be certain it isn't that of my own. I look back, one last mortified glance at the glass full of translucent orange (unsure of myself and what I am pursuing) and the glass runs clear.

Then, everything is open. I understand and know and am. The staircase comes easy. I can hear her breathing not a flight away. I should be terrified, but fear barters with lust and I acquiesce. Perhaps even, I love her.

Each plank, each nail, each bit of yesterday beneath me as I make my way upward. She is quiet now. The door glides open, her smell permeating my everything. I know her rhythm. A set of blonde locks perched precariously on a sullen pillow, the waning moon somewhere ethereal, helping no one. She is aware. She is vibrant. She is alive.

My restraint abandoned, I jaunt, and with a zeal I didn't know I was capable of accessing. Then, hearing the despondent blank whimpers and ruffles of sheets not ruffled enough, I take heed just for a moment and the moment is blaring, screaming risk be damned.

Mindless yet courteous, my nails reach for the frills of her comforter. Lifting with great caution, I find a place. She knows I am there. Employing a well-trained maneuver my hip settles near, drawn to her warmth. I find myself beside her, my angel in a feathered shroud. She undulates beneath the ivory waves I've broken and we find solace between our knotting fingers.

*Originally published as "Vodka and Scrambled Eggs" by *eFiction Publishing 2013*

ACKNOWLEDGEMENTS

I would like to thank first and foremost my editor James Hutcheson, without whom this would be even more of a mess. I'd also like to thank my family for putting up with all this nonsense and supporting its continuation.

Special thanks to the following San Francisco bay area bars and their kindly staff for providing essential sustenance and inspiration: The Old Pro, Fly Bar, McTeagues, Rogue Brewery, and The Patio.

Interview with author Robert S. Gerleman:

What inspired you to write your first book?

"When I wrote *Damned If I Do*, I was in my early twenties and had been confronted with the suicides of several of, my peers. I couldn't understand why. So, I did a little research and found that there was a huge spike in the suicide rate of suburban males in their mid-to-late-twenties. This was in part attributed to the early stages of economic collapse that lead to mass firings of the recently employed. Young men who had, sadly, found themselves de-fined by their careers, what they could provide, etc. felt that along with the loss of their jobs went self-worth. I wanted to write something that showed the darkness of this struggle for purpose but also that we can find reasons for living in the very fundamentals of life that got lost somewhere in the 'pursuit of happiness'; the love and spirit of those we surround ourselves with."

How did you come up with the title?

"Ha, actually, I was sitting at a breakfast nook with an old friend of mine. Sarah. And while explaining the plot of the book to her (at the time titled "Hopeful for Never") she said quite knowingly, 'so it's sort of a damned if I do, damned if I don't situation?'.

Do you have a specific writing style?

"I'd like to think I combine the terse, straightforward nature of Hemmingway's prose with the fast paced staccato of Bret Easton Ellis. Though I don't think I possess the bravado of the former nor the knack for dialogue of the latter."

What books have influenced your life most?

Less Than Zero really gave me that Ah-hah moment that I think Fitzgerald said he experienced after reading some of the English novelist Hugh Walpole. He said something like 'If this fellow can get away with it as an author, I can too.' Not that I think Ellis is anything short of incredible. But something about his tone and the frankness of increasingly unreliable characters really spoke to me. Woke something up I guess.

If you had to choose, which writer would you consider a mentor?

Yea, again Ellis for sure and to a lesser extent authors Nick Hornby, Hunter S., Jonathan Ames, a touch of Bukowski, and most recently, Simon Van Booy. Simply mind blowing, that guy [booy].

What book are you reading now?

Lately, I've been reading debut novels from contemporary authors as well as some of the old favorites. I have Joshua Ferris' novel *Then We Came to the End* on my desk right now, and under that is Jack Kerouac's *The Sea is my Brother*. And I just finished reading *American Spirit* by Kennedy, which was great. He constructed quite a voice in that book, great relationship between narrative and protagonist. Something like watching a hand try to grab itself in the mirror. Not to get too poetic.

What are your current projects?

I've got one in the chamber. A collaborative piece I'm working on with my friend James (Hutcheson) who is also an author as well as my editor. And, my next solo novel is of course 'under construction'. Between that and a few side projects, I'm struggling with the timeline. But most likely you'll see the collaborative work first. In the next year, Maybe.

What is the hardest part of writing a book?

Format. Editing. Trying to get over the fear of people actually reading it. Oh fiction!

Do you have any advice for other writers?

Forget every piece of advice you've ever gotten from a fellow writer. I think someone else might have said that one, oh well.

— **Megan Drescher**
CellFire 12/12/13

ABOUT THE AUTHOR

Robert Gerleman was born in Palo Alto, CA. He graduated from Humboldt State University with a degree in English and writing practices. Robert later returned to his hometown of Palo Alto to attend the Writer's Studio at Stanford University. His first novel *Damned If I Do, Damned If I Don't* was published shortly thereafter. *Nothing Really Happens* is his second major work. For more information, please visit his website:

www.robswriting.com.